W9-AOZ-602

Our Teacher's Having a Baby

This book may not leave the Offices and if borrowed must be returned within 7 days

Archive Collection

REFERENCE LIBRARY * HOUGHTON MIFFLIN CO. * BOSTON, MASS.

Our Teacher's Having a Baby

by EVE BUNTING

pictures by

Diane de Groat

CLARION BOOKS

New York

Clarion Books
a Houghton Mifflin Company imprint
215 Park Avenue South, New York, NY 10003
Text copyright © 1992 by Eve Bunting
Illustrations copyright © 1992 by Diane de Groat
All rights reserved.
For information about permission to reproduce selections from this
book, write to Permissions, Houghton Mifflin Company,
215 Park Avenue South, New York, NY 10003.
Printed in the U.S.A.

www.houghtonmifflinbooks.com

Library of Congress Cataloging-in-Publication Data
Bunting, Eve, 1928–
Our teacher's having a baby / by Eve Bunting ; illustrated by
Diane de Groat.
p. cm.
Summary: As the months pass during first-grade teacher Mrs. Neal's
pregnancy, her class gets involved writing letters to the baby, thinking up
possible names for it, and designing a baby room on the bulletin board.
ISBN 0-395-60470-2   PA ISBN 0-618-11138-7
[1. Babies—Fiction. 2. Schools—Fiction.] I. De Groat, Diane, ill.
II. Title.
PZ7.B91527Ou   1992
[E]—dc20   91-16994
CIP
AC

WOZ 10 9 8

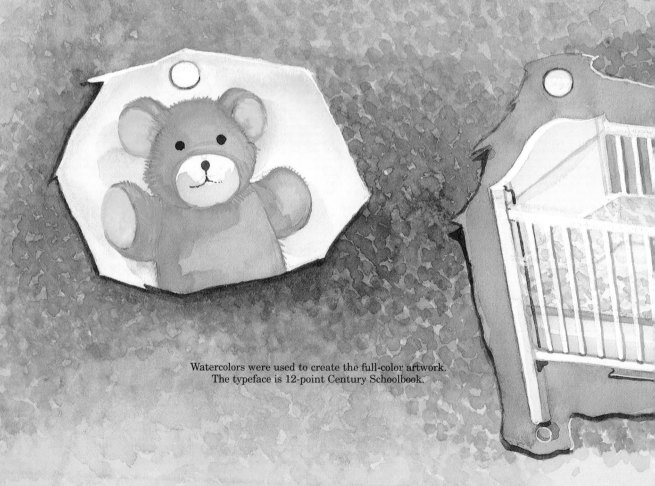

Watercolors were used to create the full-color artwork.
The typeface is 12-point Century Schoolbook.

To first-graders
Kelan Ackerman
and Dana Bunting
who helped with this book.

————

The illustrator wishes to thank the
children and staff at the Roaring
Brook School for their help in
making this book.

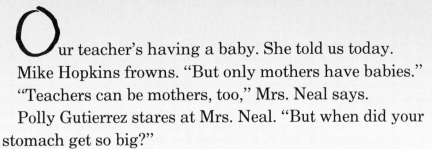

Our teacher's having a baby. She told us today.

Mike Hopkins frowns. "But only mothers have babies."

"Teachers can be mothers, too," Mrs. Neal says.

Polly Gutierrez stares at Mrs. Neal. "But when did your stomach get so big?"

Mrs. Neal blows out her cheeks to make herself funny-fat all over. The ends of her hair quiver. She pulls her long shirt tight across her front. "It has been getting this way for a while. You just didn't notice."

Polly G. rushes up and puts a sticker on Mrs. Neal's shirt, right on the stretched-out part. It says:

HAVE A NICE DAY.

"It's for the baby," Polly G. explains.

Soon Mrs. Neal's shirt is a mess of stickers.

At recess Polly G. and Janice D'Amato and I go in the corner of the playground to compare stomachs. Ours aren't very interesting.

We all think it's great that Mrs. Neal is having a baby. Linda Chen's mom had a baby last year and Cathy Kerr has twin baby sisters. But Mrs. Neal is our teacher, and that's different.

Mrs. Neal reads us books about baby animals and how they get born.

We go around the block on a nature walk to see the trees and plants.

"Everything that lives has been born, one way or the other," Mrs. Neal says.

11

Mr. Blair, who teaches sixth grade, invites us into his room to visit their white rabbit, Fluffy. Fluffy has four baby bunnies.

"When the offspring get older, we each get to borrow one on weekends," a sixth-grade boy tells us. He sounds very superior. I think "offspring" is a superior word for "babies."

"Maybe *you'll* have four offspring, Mrs. Neal," Mike Hopkins says. "Then we can borrow them on weekends."

Mrs. Neal makes a face. "*Four?* Give me a break, Mike!"

We write letters on our computer. Mine goes:

> *Dear Baby:*
> *My name is Samantha. I'm the one who gave you the*
> *butterfly sticker. I hope you are well.*

Mrs. Neal saves the letters to give to the baby later.

We talk about names we like and Mrs. Neal prints them on the blackboard.

"Should we be thinking of boys' names or girls' names?" Janice D'Amato asks. "Which kind of baby are you going to have?"

Mrs. Neal smiles. "I don't know. It's more fun to be surprised. So why don't you give me a selection."

We select "Daffodil," because daffodils come in the spring and so will the baby. In March.

And "Neil," because if it's a boy "Neil Neal" would be very distinguished.

We like "Abracadabra," too. That's the name of Mike Hopkins's boa constrictor. But when we say it together the name rolls like a drum:

AB-RA-CA-DAAAAAB-RA

It's so nice.

Every day in the music room we walk in a circle and sing extra loud so the baby can hear:

The King of France and fifty thousand men
Marched up a hill and then marched down again.

Mrs. Neal says the baby marches too, inside of her.
"Does it tickle?" Cathy Kerr asks.
Mrs. Neal giggles. "A little. But at least babies don't wear sneakers. Or boots."

We're designing a baby room on our bulletin board. We cut out magazine pictures of a crib, a dresser, and a big rocking chair so Mrs. Neal can sit when she reads bedtime stories.

She has brought a calendar from home. We cross off the days till March and groan and moan. "It's *so-ooo* hard to wait!"

Mrs. Neal groans and moans, too. "*So-ooo* hard!"

19

Then, one day in February, Mrs. Neal isn't at school. The principal is in our room.

We're excited and nervous.

"Did the baby get born?" It's scary to ask the principal questions, but we have to know.

"Yes," he says. "It came a little early. It's a girl."

We whoop and clap, and the principal doesn't even tell us to be quiet. "Her name is Isabel," he says.

"Oh."

"Well."

We decide we like "Isabel" a lot. We decide "Isabel Neal" is very distinguished. In fact, we wish we'd selected it.

The next day we get a substitute teacher. Her name is Mrs. Boskie and she's all right. But she isn't *our* teacher.

"What if Mrs. Neal never comes back?" Polly G.'s eyes are wide and frightened.

We hadn't thought of that.

"She will," we say. "She will." If we say it enough times it's sure to happen.

One Friday we get a message. Mrs. Neal will come to visit on Monday. She will bring Isabel.

"To visit," Polly G. repeats. "Only to visit."

Still, we're happy.

On Monday Mrs. Boskie has a hard time getting us to settle down.

She helps us print a banner that says WELCOME.

We make baby drawings and pin them around the room. They're all called Isabel. They all have pop eyes and a corkscrew curl on top.

Mike Hopkins keeps peering out the window.

"Here they are," he yells at last. We crowd beside him.

Mrs. Neal is carrying a pink baby basket that's stuck all over with our stickers.

We swarm around her for a first glimpse.

"Wow!" I say. "She's exactly like our Isabel drawings!"

She yawns a big yawn and that makes us laugh.

Mike Hopkins is excited. "The inside of her mouth looks just like Abracadabra's. Except he has two fangs and she doesn't have any."

We are *so* insulted. But Mrs. Neal giggles. "Oh, Mike. I have missed you!"

Of course, he is the one who asks, "Will you ever be our teacher again?"

We all stand very quietly.

Mrs. Neal looks at us and says, "Oh." It's as if she has suddenly realized something. "I need to be with my baby all the time for a while," she tells us. "But then I can leave her with a sitter while I'm at school. I'll be back. You guys are important, too."

"We were afraid . . ." I begin.

"You were? I'm sorry." She smooths my bangs. "I told you teachers can be mothers. I should have told you mothers can be teachers, too."

I smile. "I guess mothers can be anything."

"That's right, Samantha." Her voice is very soft. "Now. Would you like a closer look at Isabel?" She lifts the baby up.

"Mrs. Neal," I say, "you really do have a beautiful offspring!"

"A warm—but unsentimental—story about the excitement, anticipation, and anxieties experienced by a first-grade class whose teacher has a baby during the school year. The children's questions and comments, the teacher's good-humored responses, and the way this event becomes a focus for activities makes not only a good story but an excellent set of lesson plans for pregnant teachers!"

—*Kirkus Reviews*

"Bunting's wise and wonderful tale deserves its place on every school and public library shelf. . . . De Groat's warm watercolor illustrations portray a nurturing and joy-filled classroom. She successfully reflects all the emotions of the action from excited anticipation to complete joy to worried concern. An excellent collaboration."

—*School Library Journal*

$5.95

ISBN 0-618-11138-7

90000

9 780618 111381

1-11057
0301
Cover illustrations copyright © 1992 by Diane de Groat

THE WIMP

Kathy Caple